Grain of
Redemption

Books by Judd R. Johnson

Grain of Redemption

Grain of
Redemption

Judd R. Johnson

www.ideacreationspress.com

"SILAS"

Of the Forest, a woodland dweller.

Latin "Silvanus" meaning "wood" or Forrest"

Form of Silouanos, related to Seila or Saul

"Asked for" or "Prayed For".

Conveys themes of Nature, Loyalty, Wisdom and steadfastness

This story was shaped by quiet endurance, unseen sacrifice, and the belief that nothing given in love is ever wasted, so I would like to dedicate this book to:

Those who stood when it would have been easier to fall.

For those who gave what could not be replaced.

And for the generations who may never understand the fire, only the shelter it made possible.

Its redemption belongs to anyone who has learned that faith is not proven by what is spared, but by what is faithfully given.

PROLOGUE

BEFORE THE STORM HAD A NAME

There are truths that cannot be taught.

They must be lived into understanding.

Before Silas knew the weight of an axe, before his hands learned the patience of grain and edge, before the forest ever asked anything costly of him, there was a knowing that settled quietly in his bones: some things are entrusted, not owned.

He felt it as a boy, walking the valley in the early hours when the world had not yet decided what it would demand of the day. Mist clung low to the ground. Light moved carefully through branches. The forest breathed as one body—old, enduring, unconcerned with haste.

Nothing was yet broken.

Nothing was yet tested.

And yet, everything was already preparing.

Silas did not understand then that storms leave their signatures long before they arrive. That fire announces itself first in dryness, in neglect, in small choices overlooked because life feels stable. He did not know that strength is always formed in advance, quietly, patiently, out of sight.

He only knew that when he placed his hand against a tree, something ancient answered back.

Not with words, but with steadiness.

It was the kind of steadiness that does not promise protection from loss—only the assurance that loss is not the end of the story. The kind that does not explain suffering, but teaches you how to stand inside it without losing who you are.

This is the kind of story that grows slowly.

It does not begin with fire.

It begins with soil.

With unseen roots learning where to reach when the surface offers nothing. With rings forming long before anyone stops to count them. With a quiet faithfulness that looks ordinary until it is the only thing left standing.

This is not a story about saving what we love from every storm.

It is a story about what remains when the storm has passed.

And it begins, as all enduring things do,

Before anyone is watching—

Before the cost is known—

When care is still simple,

And faith has not yet been asked

To prove how much it trusts the ground beneath it.

CHAPTER ONE

THE SILENCE BEFORE BECOMING

Silas learned silence before he learned speech.

Not the absence of sound, but the kind that lives underneath it — the stillness that holds everything together. It was there in the valley where he was born, in the long pauses between wind and birdsong, in the way the forest seemed to wait rather than hurry.

His grandfather used to say the land remembered those who listened.

The old man was a woodsman like the men before him, hands knotted with age and resin, voice worn thin from use. He believed trees spoke in ways that words never could, and that if you hurried past them, they would let you — but if you stayed, truly stayed, they would shape you.

Silas followed him often as a boy, walking a half-step behind, matching his pace to the rhythm of boots that knew the ground by heart. They rarely spoke. There was no need. The forest did not belong to conversation; it belonged to attention.

When his grandfather died, Silas inherited not tools, but posture — the way a man stands when he does not seek to conquer what he touches.

Silas was twelve when the storm came that changed everything.

It tore through the valley in the dark hours before dawn, a violent, restless thing that bent trees until they groaned and ripped branches free as if testing the limits of devotion. When morning broke, the forest looked wounded. Leaves lay scattered like torn letters. The ground was raw and exposed.

Silas walked alone that morning, drawn by something he could not name.

That was when he saw the sapling.

It stood near the edge of a small rise, bent nearly double, its roots clawing at the air. Mud streaked its base. It should have fallen. Everything about it said unfinished.

Silas felt a tightening in his chest — a recognition that startled him.

The tree looked the way he felt when grief first entered his home.

Exposed. Upright only by effort. Still alive.

He knelt.

The soil was cold and heavy in his hands as he pressed it back into place. He worked slowly, packing the earth firm around the roots, steadying the trunk with care that bordered on reverence. He cut a thin stake from fallen wood and anchored the sapling against the wind.

No one told him to do this.

No one would praise him for it.

But as he worked, something quiet settled in him — a knowing that this moment mattered far beyond its size.

"Stand," he whispered boldly, unsure whether the word was meant for the tree or himself.

Silas returned often after that.

He told no one. Some things, he sensed, were not meant to be shared yet. He cleared weeds, checked the soil, adjusted the stake when storms loosened it. He did not overprotect it. He had learned from watching his elders that too much shelter breeds weakness.

Faith, he was beginning to understand, was not control.

It was trust expressed through care.

Seasons passed. The sapling grew, slowly and stubbornly. Each year it leaned a little less. Each winter it endured more. Silas marked time not by age, but by height — the day the tree reached his chest, then his shoulder, then rose above him entirely.

When his father died suddenly — taken by illness with no warning — Silas returned to the tree and sat with his back against its trunk until the sun fell away. He did not pray with words. He did not ask why.

He stayed.

And staying, he would later realize, was the beginning of belief.

Years turned Silas into a man.

He became a carpenter like his fathers before him, shaping wood into things meant to outlast moments — tables that gathered families, doors that guarded thresholds, beams that bore weight quietly. He married, raised children, buried disappointments he never spoke aloud.

And through it all, the tree grew.

It became the tallest in the valley, its branches spreading wide, its roots deep and unseen. Birds nested in it instinctively. Children played beneath it. Travelers rested in its shade without knowing why they felt peace there.

Silas brought his own son to the tree when the boy was small.

"Why this one?" the child asked.

Silas rested his hand against the bark, feeling the solid truth beneath the scars.

"Because it stayed," he said. "And because someone once helped it stand."

The boy pressed his palm to the trunk, as Silas once had, and smiled.

In that moment, Silas understood something his grandfather had tried to teach him without words:

Legacy is not what we leave behind.

It is what we tend long enough to pass on.

As the years deepened, Silas noticed how the tree had changed him.

When storms came to his life — and they did — he did not curse them. He let them shape him. When grief returned, he did not flee it. He rooted deeper. When joy arrived, he offered shelter without fear of loss.

The tree did not teach him how to avoid suffering.

It taught him how to endure it faithfully.

And Silas, without realizing it, became a reflection of the very thing he had once knelt to save.

By the time the drought began — the long one that would lead to fire — the tree stood as a living witness to endurance. People spoke of it with reverence now, though few remembered when it had been weak.

Silas remembered.

He always would.

Because long before the flames, before the fall, before the transformation yet to come — there was this quiet beginning.

A boy kneeling in the dirt.

A tree refusing to give up.

A faith taking root long before it had a name.

CHAPTER TWO

RINGS BENEATH THE BARK

Silas learned early that the most important work was never visible.

His father used to say the strength of a beam could not be judged by its polish. You had to know where it came from—how it grew, what winds tested it, whether it had been rushed or allowed to take its time. A piece of wood could look sound and still fail under the weight if its years had been easy.

"Soft seasons make weak timber," his father would say, not unkindly.

Silas did not understand this fully until much later.

The tree's growth was slow in the beginning, so gradual that it was easy to believe nothing was happening at all.

One year it gained little height. Another year it thickened but did not stretch. Its progress did not follow the eager patterns of other trees that raced skyward only to crack under their own ambition.

This one lingered.

Its roots, Silas noticed, seemed to prefer darkness. They moved downward, not outward, threading through stone and compacted earth as though searching for something deeper than water alone. During dry years, when neighboring saplings yellowed and failed, this tree endured with quiet determination.

Silas began to understand that the tree was being formed for something weighty.

There were years in Silas's own life that mirrored this slow resistance.

After his father's death, the house grew quieter in ways that felt unnatural. The tools remained, hanging in their places, but the hands that had taught him their use were gone. Silas stepped into responsibilities without ceremony—providing, fixing, deciding—roles that settled on his shoulders without asking permission.

He married young, believing love alone would carry him through what he did not yet know how to face. For a time, it did. Then children came, along with worry, scarcity, and the long ache of unanswered prayers.

Some nights, Silas sat at the table long after the others had gone to sleep, staring at his hands as if they might explain what his heart could not. He wondered if faith was meant to feel so heavy. If obedience was always this quiet. If endurance was mistaken for absence.

And still, like the tree, he remained.

When his son was born, Silas felt a fear he had never known.

Not fear of harm—but fear of inheritance.

He wondered what unseen rings he would pass on. What griefs, unspoken doubts, and hardened habits might settle into the grain of another life without ever being named.

He brought the boy to the tree often, setting him down at its base while he worked nearby. The child would reach for the bark, tracing the ridges with curious fingers, pressing his ear against the trunk as if listening for something hidden.

"What do you hear?" Silas asked once.

The boy thought for a moment. "It sounds like breathing."

Silas looked at the tree and felt something loosen in his chest.

Years layered themselves quietly, like rings no one would see until the end.

There were seasons of abundance when laughter filled the house and work flowed easily. There were others when money was scarce and patience thinner than Silas cared to admit. Arguments rose and fell like storms—some passing cleanly, others leaving damage that took years to mend.

Through it all, the tree continued its slow becoming.

Storms bent it but did not break it. Winters scarred it with ice. Summers tested it with thirst. Each hardship pressed into its core, tightening the grain, strengthening what could not be seen.

Silas began to recognize the pattern not as punishment, but preparation.

One evening, after a particularly hard season, Silas brought his son into the workshop. The boy was old enough now to hold tools, though his hands still trembled with uncertainty.

Silas selected a rough piece of wood and split it open along the grain. The inside revealed tight, uneven rings—years of struggle etched plainly into the heart.

"This tree lived through drought," Silas said. "See how close the rings are? It didn't grow fast. It grew strong."

The boy ran his fingers over the exposed heartwood. "Is that bad?"

Silas shook his head. "It's why it lasted."

He did not say what he was thinking—that the hardest years of his life had shaped him more than the easy ones ever could. That faith, like wood, revealed its truth only when opened.

As the tree grew taller, it began to draw attention.

People spoke of its height, its resilience, its commanding presence. Some asked Silas how it had grown so strong when others had failed.

He smiled and answered simply, "It was given time."

But privately, he knew the truth was deeper.

The tree had been allowed to suffer without abandonment.

It had been supported without being spared.

It had been shaped, not rescued.

Silas wondered if this was how God worked as well.

There came a year when the rains did not return.

The soil cracked. The streams thinned. Crops failed. Anxiety settled over the valley like a low fog. Silas felt the familiar tightening in his chest—the sense that another season of endurance was being asked of him.

He walked to the tree and placed his hand against its trunk.

It stood firm.

Not untouched by the drought, but not defeated by it either. Its leaves were fewer, its growth slowed, but its posture remained steady.

Silas closed his eyes and whispered a prayer without words.

Teach me to stand like this, he thought.

Teach my son to root where storms cannot reach.

He did not yet know what fire awaited them all.

But the rings were already forming.

And one day, when the tree's life would be revealed in grain and scar alike, those hidden years would tell a story not of ease—but of endurance worthy of being passed on.

CHAPTER THREE

A SHADOW WIDE ENOUGH FOR MANY

There came a time when the tree no longer belonged to Silas alone.

He noticed it first in small, almost forgettable ways. A traveler resting beneath its branches longer than necessary. A shepherd guiding his flock toward its shade rather than pressing on. Children drifting instinctively toward its roots, as though drawn by something older than curiosity.

The tree had begun to gather people.

Silas watched this quietly, uncertain at first how he felt about it. There was a possessiveness in him he did not like to admit—a sense that what he had tended in secret was now being claimed by the world. But the feeling did not last. It could not survive the sight of weary bodies finding rest, or the sound of laughter rising where there had once been only wind.

The tree had grown wide enough to shelter others.

And Silas sensed that this, too, was part of its calling.

The valley was not an easy place to live.

Seasons were unpredictable. Work was demanding. Loss arrived often and without explanation. People learned to endure, but endurance had a way of hollowing them out if they endured alone.

The tree became a place where that loneliness softened.

Neighbors began to meet there—not by plan, but by pattern. Someone would arrive to rest, another to pass the time, another simply because they felt unsettled and did not know why. Conversations unfolded slowly, like leaves opening after rain. No one spoke loudly. Something about the place discouraged hurry.

Silas would sometimes sit nearby, repairing tools or shaping small pieces of wood, listening without intruding. He noticed how people spoke more honestly beneath the branches. How grief found language there. How joy did not feel foolish.

The tree did not offer answers.

It offered presence.

One afternoon, a woman named Mara arrived with her children in tow.

Her husband had died the winter before, taken by sickness that moved faster than prayer. Since then, she had grown thin with effort and worry, carrying grief like a pack she could not set down.

She sat at the base of the tree and wept openly, her children pressing close, unsure what to do with tears they could not stop. Silas watched from a distance, unsure whether to approach.

The tree swayed gently overhead.

After a long while, Mara leaned back against the trunk, exhaustion overtaking sorrow. Her breathing slowed. Her shoulders lowered. She did not smile—but she rested.

Later, when she rose to leave, she pressed her hand to the bark and whispered something Silas could not hear.

From that day on, she returned often. Stronger each time.

Silas began to see himself reflected in the tree more clearly than ever before.

He, too, had become a place where others came— neighbors seeking counsel, young men asking about work, elders wanting help with repairs they could no longer manage. He did not seek this role. It found him.

At times, it felt heavy.

There were evenings when he returned home drained, having carried stories he could not fix. His wife noticed the way his silence deepened, the way his shoulders bore invisible weight.

"You don't have to hold everyone," she told him once, gently.

Silas nodded, but he did not step away.

Because something inside him recognized the truth he had learned from the tree:

Shelter is costly, but it is holy.

He brought his son to the tree more often now, not just to sit, but to watch.

"Why do people come here?" the boy asked one day, tracing shapes in the dirt with a stick.

Silas considered the question carefully. "Because it's strong enough to share."

The boy looked up at the wide canopy. "Will it ever get tired?"

Silas smiled sadly. "Everything that gives does."

The answer unsettled him more than he let on.

Storms came that tested the tree's growing role.

One night, a violent wind tore through the valley, driving rain sideways and snapping weaker limbs throughout the forest. People fled their homes, seeking whatever cover they could find.

Some ran to the tree.

Silas stood beneath its branches with others, the wind roaring like judgment overhead. The tree bent deeply, its massive trunk groaning under pressure. Branches whipped violently, but they did not break.

As the storm passed, Silas rested his hand against the bark, feeling the slow, steady pulse beneath.

It had held.

Not rigidly—but faithfully.

He realized then that the tree's strength was not in resisting the storm, but in absorbing it on behalf of others.

And something in that realization frightened him.

Because faith, he was learning, was not merely about standing firm for oneself.

It was about becoming a refuge.

And refuges are eventually worn down.

Silas wondered if this was why the tree had grown so slowly—why its roots had gone so deep. It had been preparing not just to endure storms, but to carry others through them.

He thought of the quiet years. The droughts. The tight rings hidden beneath bark.

None of it had been wasted.

As the seasons turned, the tree became a marker in the valley.

Directions were given by it. Stories were told beneath it. Children grew up knowing it as a constant, an unspoken promise that something solid remained.

Few remembered when it had been small.

Fewer still knew it had once nearly fallen.

Silas remembered.

And as he watched his son begin to offer quiet help to others—sharing food, listening longer than required, standing patiently with those who struggled—Silas felt a mixture of pride and awe.

The legacy was already passing on.

Not through instruction.

Through example.

That night, Silas knelt at the base of the tree alone.

He rested his forehead against the bark, the way he had when grief first taught him how to stay. He did not ask for strength. He did not ask for ease.

He asked only this:

Let me be shaped enough to shelter others

Without losing what roots me to You.

Above him, the branches whispered softly.

And though the answer did not come in words, Silas felt it settle deep within him:

What is given in love is never taken in vain.

CHAPTER FOUR

WHEN HEIGHT DRAWS THE WIND

What rose highest in the valley learned first what it meant to be tested.

Silas understood this long before the storms returned in force. It was a truth the forest whispered often: the taller something grows, the more it is exposed. Wind does not seek out the low places. It looks for what dares to stand above the rest.

The tree had become impossible to ignore.

From nearly anywhere in the valley, its crown could be seen lifting above the surrounding forest, a dark silhouette against the sky. Travelers used it as a guide. Children used it as a meeting place. Elders measured the passing years by how much wider its shadow had grown.

With that attention came a quiet pressure.

Silas felt it in himself as well.

People looked to him now—not just for craft or labor, but for counsel. His words carried weight whether he intended them to or not. Silence, once a refuge, became something others tried to read for meaning. When he spoke, people listened. When he hesitated, they noticed.

It unsettled him.

He had never wanted to be seen this way. Like the tree, he had grown simply by remaining faithful to what was given to him. Yet faithfulness, he was learning, sometimes places a man where visibility is unavoidable.

The first great storm of that season came at dusk.

The air thickened throughout the day, heavy and watchful. Birds fell silent early. Even the forest seemed to hold its breath. Silas felt the familiar tightening in his chest—the quiet warning that something was coming.

By nightfall, the wind arrived.

It howled through the valley with a hunger that rattled doors and shook the earth itself. Rain followed, driven sideways, striking bark and stone with relentless force. Trees bent and groaned. Branches snapped and fell, unseen but unmistakable in their breaking.

Silas pulled on his coat and stepped outside.

He did not know why he went to the tree. He only knew he had to see it.

The wind struck the great tree first.

It bent deeply, far more than Silas had ever seen, its massive trunk swaying with a violence that made his breath catch. Branches lashed wildly, leaves tearing free and vanishing into the dark.

For the first time, Silas felt afraid for it.

Not the fleeting worry of past storms—but a deeper fear, the kind that recognizes the cost of standing where many depend on you.

He stood at a distance, rain soaking through him, powerless to help. All he could do was witness.

The tree did not resist the wind.

It yielded.

It bowed so far Silas thought it would snap, yet each time it returned—upright, though shaken. Roots held. Fiber flexed. Years of hidden strengthening revealed themselves in motion rather than stillness.

Silas understood then that endurance was not static.

It was dynamic obedience.

By morning, the storm had passed.

The valley bore its marks—fallen limbs, split trunks, scattered debris. Several trees lay broken, their roots torn free where shallow ground could not hold them.

The great tree still stood.

But it was changed.

A massive branch had torn loose near the crown, leaving a jagged wound where wood was exposed to the air. Sap bled slowly, dark and steady, like a quiet offering.

Silas approached carefully, laying his hand against the wounded place.

The bark was warm beneath his palm.

Something in him ached.

Word of the damage spread quickly.

People came to see for themselves, murmuring in relief that the tree had survived. Some spoke of cutting it back, of trimming its height to spare it future harm. Others argued it should be left alone, that interfering now would be an act of fear rather than wisdom.

Silas listened without speaking.

He knew the truth was not simple.

To lessen the tree's reach might protect it—but it would also reduce the shelter it provided. To leave it as it was meant accepting that more storms would come, and that each one would cost something.

That night, Silas sat alone beneath the branches long after the others had gone.

He rested his back against the trunk and closed his eyes.

I did not ask for this height, he thought.

I did not seek this weight.

And yet, it had come.

In the weeks that followed, Silas noticed subtle changes.

The tree's growth slowed. Its energy seemed redirected inward, strengthening what had been strained. New shoots appeared around the wound—not hiding it, but growing in response to it.

Silas saw the same pattern in himself.

The storm had left him quieter, more deliberate. He chose words carefully now, aware of their reach. He began to understand that leadership was not about answers, but about steadiness under pressure.

His son noticed too.

"You don't rush anymore," the boy said one evening as they worked together.

Silas smiled faintly. "Rushing breaks things that need time."

Another storm came later that year, though less fierce.

Again, the tree bent. Again, it held.

But Silas knew now that each test left its mark. Faith was not proven once. It was refined repeatedly.

He thought of the unseen rings beneath the bark, of the scars that would one day tell the tree's full story. He thought of his own life—of losses endured, responsibilities accepted, prayers spoken without certainty of response.

None of it had been wasted.

One evening, Silas brought his son to the tree just as the sun dipped low, casting long shadows across the valley.

"Do you see how it leans?" Silas asked.

The boy nodded.

"It looks like it might fall."

Silas placed a hand over his son's shoulder. "It only looks that way because you're watching closely now."

The boy was quiet for a long moment.

"Will it always have to stand like this?"

Silas did not answer right away.

"No," he said finally. "One day it will rest. But until then, it stands so others don't have to fall."

As twilight settled, Silas felt a strange peace.

He understood now that height was not a reward—it was a responsibility. One that came with exposure, with cost, with sacrifice that would never be fully seen or thanked.

And yet—

This was the place faith had grown him into.

The wind would come again. He knew that. For the tree. For himself. For the generations watching quietly from below.

But the roots were deep.

And for now, that was enough.

CHAPTER FIVE

THE WORK OF HANDS AND HEART

There was a rhythm to Silas's workshop that had nothing to do with clocks.

It lived in the rise and fall of breath, in the steady pull of the plane along grain, in the pause before a cut was made. The space smelled of sawdust and oil, of time worn into usefulness. Light entered through a single high window, settling softly on the bench where Silas worked as generations before him had done.

Here, he felt closest to understanding prayer.

Not the spoken kind—but the kind shaped through attention and obedience. The kind that asked not for outcomes, but alignment.

Wood did not lie.

It revealed itself slowly, honestly. Grain showed where a tree had struggled, where it had grown fast or tight, where storms had twisted it inward. Silas learned to read these signs the way others read scripture—carefully, humbly, knowing that misinterpretation led to fracture.

Force broke wood.

Patience transformed it.

Silas had learned the craft from his father, who learned it from his own, each man passing down not just technique, but restraint. The first lesson had never been how to cut—but how to wait.

"Let the wood tell you what it wants to be," his father had said, placing a rough board in Silas's hands when he was still a boy. "Your job is not to conquer it. Your job is to listen."

Silas had not understood then how much of life that rule would govern.

In recent years, he found himself lingering longer in the workshop, especially when the world outside felt heavy. There were seasons when prayer felt thin, when faith seemed distant and obligation felt louder than conviction.

On those days, Silas returned to the bench.

He shaped small things then—bowls, boxes, simple pieces meant for use rather than admiration. He let his hands move slowly, deliberately, allowing the act of making to quiet the questions he did not know how to voice.

Sometimes his son worked beside him, silent but attentive, learning through watching rather than instruction. Silas noticed how the boy's hands hesitated before cuts, how his eyes followed the grain instinctively.

The legacy was already forming.

One evening, as the light faded and the work slowed, the boy grew frustrated.

The piece he was shaping split unexpectedly, a thin crack running against the grain where he had rushed the blade. He stared at it, jaw tight, shame rising quickly.

"I ruined it," he said.

Silas stepped closer, turning the piece gently in his hands.

"No," he said softly. "You revealed it."

The boy looked confused.

"This crack was already there," Silas continued. "You just found it too quickly. That happens when you push instead of follow."

The boy swallowed hard. "Can it be fixed?"

Silas nodded. "Most things can. But they won't be what you first imagined."

They worked together then, adjusting the design, letting the flaw become part of the final form rather than something to be hidden.

Later, as the boy swept shavings from the floor, Silas felt the weight of the lesson settle deeply within him.

How many times had he rushed God's shaping?

How many fractures had come not from malice—but impatience?

Silas thought often of the great tree during those quiet hours.

He saw its story written in every board he touched—the tight rings of hardship, the scars where branches once tore free, the slow, faithful growth that produced strength rather than spectacle.

The tree had never resisted shaping.

It had simply grown where it was planted, responding honestly to the conditions it was given.

Silas wondered if faith was meant to be that simple.

Not easy—but uncomplicated.

There were nights when doubt crept in quietly, uninvited.

When prayers for protection over his family felt unanswered. When the valley's growing drought stirred unease, he could not shake. When the tree's wounds from the last storm lingered longer than he liked.

In those moments, Silas would run his hand along a finished piece of wood, feeling the smoothness earned through abrasion, not avoidance.

He remembered something his grandfather once said, voice thin but certain:

"God doesn't waste pressure. He turns it into polish."

The next morning, Silas rose early and walked to the tree before work.

Sunlight filtered through the canopy, illuminating scars left by past storms. The great wound near its crown had begun to harden, sealing itself slowly, faithfully.

Silas placed his hand against the trunk and felt the familiar steadiness beneath the surface.

He did not ask for safety.

He asked for faithfulness.

Teach my hands to follow Your grain, he thought.

Even when the shape costs more than I expect.

As the season pressed on, work in the valley grew more uncertain. Crops struggled. Streams thinned further. Talk of fire drifted quietly through conversations like an unspoken warning.

Silas felt the tension building—not in panic, but in preparation.

He returned to the workshop with renewed intention, teaching his son not just how to build, but why.

"Make things that last," he said one evening. "Not because they're perfect—but because they're honest."

The boy nodded, absorbing the words without fully understanding them yet.

Someday, Silas knew, he would.

That night, as Silas closed the workshop door, he looked once more toward the tree rising dark against the sky.

It stood marked but unbowed. Scarred but generous. Shaped by forces beyond its choosing.

So much like the life he had been given.

Silas did not know what fire lay ahead—what loss or sacrifice would be required before redemption could be revealed. But he knew this:

He would meet it the same way he met the wood.

With open hands.

With patient faith.

With trust in the shaping he could not yet see.

CHAPTER SIX

THE DAY THE SKY BURNED

The fire did not come like an enemy with a face.

It came like consequence.

Weeks of drought had tightened the valley into something brittle. Leaves curled inward on themselves. Streams thinned to threads that whispered where they once sang. Even the forest seemed to move more carefully, as if each branch knew it was holding something precious and easily lost.

Silas felt it long before the smoke appeared.

There was a weight in the air that prayer did not lift, only steadied. Mornings grew strangely quiet. Birds left earlier than usual. At dusk, the horizon took on a dull, watchful hue that made Silas linger longer outside than he meant to, eyes searching the ridgelines as though expecting judgment to crest them.

When the first plume rose, it was distant enough to be dismissed.

When the second followed, thicker and darker, dismissal gave way to preparation.

The fire moved faster than anyone expected.

Wind carried it down the slopes with ruthless efficiency, feeding it dry undergrowth and years of neglect. Sirens cut through the valley like warnings too late to change what was already moving.

Silas gathered his family quickly, voice calm even as his chest tightened. They loaded what they could carry—essentials stripped down to meaning rather than memory. His son asked about the workshop. Silas shook his head.

"Things can be remade," he said. "Lives cannot."

Before leaving, Silas turned toward the forest one last time.

The great tree stood in the distance, dark against the rising smoke.

For a moment—only a moment—he considered going to it.

But fire does not negotiate with devotion.

He pressed his palm against the doorframe of his home, whispered a blessing over what would be left behind, and led his family away.

From the ridge above the valley, they watched the fire descend.

Flames leapt from crown to crown, driven by wind that seemed determined to erase. The sky darkened to an angry red, ash falling like corrupted snow. The sound was not a roar so much as a consuming breath—steady, relentless, alive.

Silas stood apart from the others, eyes fixed on the place where the great tree stood.

He could not see it now.

Smoke swallowed everything.

And in that blindness, something in him finally broke open.

Not in anger.

In surrender.

He had believed—quietly, faithfully—that some things earned protection by virtue of what they had endured. That the tree, marked by storms and years of sheltering others, would somehow be spared.

But faith, he was learning, did not work that way.

God did not bargain with suffering.

God entered it.

Silas knelt there on the ridge, ash collecting in the creases of his hands, and felt a grief deeper than loss of property or place. This was the grief of watching something holy be tested beyond recognition.

He did not ask why.

He asked only for the strength not to turn away.

The fire burned through the night.

By morning, the valley lay silent.

Smoke drifted low, heavy with the smell of endings. The forest that had once breathed life into the land now stood blackened and skeletal, its voice reduced to the soft collapse of embers surrendering to ash.

Silas returned as soon as it was safe.

He walked alone, boots sinking into warm earth, every step measured, reverent. Familiar paths had vanished. Landmarks were gone. Even the air felt different— emptied of something essential.

Then he saw it.

The great tree still stood.

But it was no longer what it had been.

Its crown was gone, burned away entirely. Bark hung split and charred, exposing heartwood scarred by flame. The place where sap once flowed freely was darkened, the life within moving slowly now, if at all.

And yet—

It had not fallen.

Silas approached carefully, laying his hand against the trunk.

It was warm. Not with life—but with memory.

The tree had absorbed the fire. It had stood long enough to shield what lay behind it, taking the worst of the heat into itself. Smaller trees nearby, those that once sheltered beneath its canopy, showed signs of survival where they should not have.

Silas sank to his knees.

He stayed there a long time.

He spoke aloud now, not caring who might hear.

"You stood," he said hoarsely. "You stood when everything burned."

He waited for something—an answer, a reassurance, a miracle.

None came.

Instead, there was only the truth settling quietly in his chest:

Some sacrifices are not meant to be prevented.

They are meant to be received.

In the days that followed, the tree weakened visibly.

Leaves did not return. New growth did not emerge. The wounds from fire deepened, not in drama, but in inevitability. Life lingered—just enough to be honored, not enough to be saved.

Others in the valley spoke of it often now, voices hushed, reverent.

"That tree saved the lower ridge."

"If it had fallen sooner—"

"We owe it everything."

Silas said nothing.

He knew gratitude came too late to preserve what mattered most.

One evening, he brought his son to the tree.

They stood together in the quiet, the forest still unfamiliar in its burned state. The boy reached for the bark and pulled his hand back quickly.

"It's still warm," he said.

Silas nodded. "Some things hold their fire longer."

The boy's voice trembled. "Is it going to die?"

Silas knelt so they were eye to eye.

"Yes," he said gently. "But not for nothing."

That night, Silas did not sleep.

He sat alone beneath the stars, which looked harsher now without the soft breath of leaves between them and the earth. He thought of the rings hidden beneath the bark—years of drought and storm, of quiet growth and unseen preparation.

He thought of his own life.

Of the ways faith had shaped him slowly, painfully, faithfully. Of the people he had sheltered. Of the cost he had not yet fully counted.

And he understood then what redemption would require.

It would not come by saving the tree.

It would come by honoring what it gave.

As dawn broke, light filtered through the broken forest, touching the great tree one last time in gold.

Silas stood and rested his hand against it.

"You will not be wasted," he whispered. "I promise."

The words felt heavier than any vow he had ever made.

But they rooted deep.

CHAPTER SEVEN

THE SLOW LETTING GO

Dying, Silas learned, was rarely loud.

It did not arrive with the drama of the fire that preceded it, nor with the finality people expected from endings. It came instead as a long, faithful retreat—a gradual loosening of what had once held fast.

The tree did not fall.

It remained standing, though each day revealed what the flames had taken. Sap no longer ran freely. Leaves did not return with the morning light. The bark darkened and cracked further, pulling away from the trunk like skin surrendering its claim.

Silas came every day.

At first, he told himself it was duty—that someone should witness the passing of something that had given so much. But soon he understood it was something else entirely.

It was love learning how to stay when nothing could be fixed.

He brought water sometimes, though he knew it would not change the outcome. He cleared debris from the base, not because the tree needed it, but because care, once learned, does not disappear simply because hope changes shape.

Silas spoke less now.

Words felt intrusive in the presence of something completing its work. Instead, he sat with his back against the trunk and listened—to the subtle creak of fibers adjusting, to the quiet settling of ash, to the sound of his own breathing slowing to match the place.

This, he realized, was a kind of prayer he had never practiced before.

Not the prayer of asking.

The prayer of accompanying.

Others came too, though not as often.

Some could not bear the sight of what had been lost. Others came briefly, offering words meant to comfort themselves more than the tree. Silas welcomed them all, but he did not rush the moment.

Grief, like growth, demanded time.

One afternoon, Mara came again, standing at a distance before approaching slowly. She placed her palm against the charred bark and closed her eyes.

"It feels wrong," she said quietly. "That something so strong could end like this."

Silas nodded. "It would be wrong," he replied, "if this were the end of the story."

She looked at him, searching his face.

"What story is left?" she asked.

Silas rested his hand against the trunk, feeling the warmth that still lingered deep within.

"The part where we remember what was given," he said. "And decide what to do with it."

His son came often now, walking beside Silas in silence that was no longer restless.

The boy watched closely as days passed, noticing changes others missed—the way the bark loosened, the subtle lean that had not been there before, the quiet resignation that marked the tree's final season.

One evening, as they sat together, the boy asked, "Does it hurt?"

Silas considered the question longer than the boy expected.

"I don't know," he said finally. "But I know it trusted the ground enough to stay standing."

The boy leaned against him, small but steady.

"I think I'd be scared," he said.

Silas wrapped an arm around his shoulders. "So am I," he admitted. "But fear doesn't mean we leave."

As weeks passed, Silas felt something shift within himself.

He had always believed faith was proven just by action—by doing, building, fixing. But now he was being taught a quieter obedience.

Stay.

Witness.

Honor.

He remembered the early years—the sapling bent and vulnerable, the storms that carved strength ring by ring, the long seasons when growth was hidden. All of it had led here, to this moment where effort gave way to reverence.

This, too, was faith.

One night, a gentle wind passed through the valley, stirring ash into the air like a soft reminder. Silas felt the tree move—not bending now, but settling, adjusting its weight as if preparing for rest.

He stood suddenly, heart tight.

"Not yet," he whispered, unsure who he was addressing.

But life does not pause at our readiness.

The tree was teaching him one final lesson.

Silas spent that night beneath the stars, refusing to leave. He watched the slow arc of the sky, thought of all the nights the tree had stood here alone, absorbing storms, offering shelter, bearing weight unseen.

Just before dawn, there was a sound—not a crash, but a deep, resonant sigh.

The tree shifted.

It did not fall then, but Silas knew.

The end was near.

In the days that followed, Silas began to prepare—not for loss, but for responsibility.

He measured carefully. He studied the grain where it showed through cracks in the bark. He traced scars left by fire and storm, memorizing their placement as one memorizes the lines of a face.

He was not planning to take the tree.

He was planning to receive it.

There was a difference.

When the tree finally fell, it did so quietly, laying itself down with the dignity of something that had finished its work.

Silas stood alone for a long time, hands at his sides, heart full and hollow all at once.

He knelt, pressing his forehead to the wood that was still warm in places.

"Thank you," he said.

And in that moment, grief did not crush him.

It consecrated him.

He understood now what redemption required.

Not denial of death.

Not rescue from loss.

But the faithful transformation of what remained.

CHAPTER EIGHT

THE HEARTWOOD KEPT

The forest felt different once the tree laid down.

Not emptier—quieter. As though something essential had finished speaking and the land itself was listening now, holding its breath in respect. Where the great tree had once stood upright, there was only sky, too wide and unfamiliar. The ground beneath bore the shape of what had rested there, pressed into ash and soil like an imprint memory refuse to let fade.

Silas did not rush.

He understood instinctively that this was not a task to be completed, but a passage to be honored.

For several days, he did nothing but sit with what remained. He walked the length of the fallen trunk slowly, hand resting against bark blackened by fire, fingers tracing the story written there—scars from storms, splits from weight borne too long, places where lightning had once kissed the crown and left it stronger rather than shattered.

This was not debris.

This was testimony.

When Silas finally brought his tools, he carried them the way one carries something sacred—quietly, deliberately, with no audience invited.

His son walked beside him, solemn now, sensing the gravity of the work ahead. The boy said nothing, but his eyes followed every movement, every pause. Silas knew this moment would live in him long after the details faded.

"You don't take everything," Silas said softly, breaking the silence. "You choose."

The boy nodded. "How do you know what to keep?"

Silas rested his palm against the exposed heartwood where fire had split the trunk open. The grain there was dark and dense, rings pressed close together—years of drought, years of endurance etched plainly into the wood.

"You keep what endured the most," he said. "Not because it survived easier—but because it carried more."

They worked slowly.

Silas cut away what had been damaged beyond honoring—not with frustration, but with acceptance. Some wood had done its work already and needed to return to the soil. He let it go without regret.

Other pieces, though scarred, were sound.

The heartwood revealed itself reluctantly, as though waiting to be asked rather than taken. It was heavier than expected, dense with memory, resistant to haste. Silas adjusted his pace, allowing the wood to lead.

His son helped where he could, lifting smaller sections, brushing ash aside, learning the difference between removal and reverence.

"Why not make many things?" the boy asked at one point. "There's enough."

Silas shook his head. "There's only enough for one thing that matters."

As they worked, people from the valley came quietly, standing at a respectful distance. No one spoke loudly. No one asked questions.

They understood, even if they could not explain it.

This was not salvage.

This was stewardship.

Mara came with her children, leaving food nearby without comment. Others brought water, blankets, presence. The community gathered not to claim, but to witness—drawn together once more by the same force that had gathered them beneath the living tree.

Silas felt the weight of it then—not as pressure, but as trust.

The tree had sheltered many.

Now its legacy would be shaped on behalf of many.

When the heartwood was finally separated, Silas rested his hands on it and closed his eyes.

He felt the truth settle fully at last:

The tree had not been taken by fire.

It had been offered through it.

Just as faith is not proven by what we keep, but by what we give without certainty of return.

That night, Silas and his son carried the chosen wood back to the workshop.

The familiar space felt altered in its presence, as though the walls themselves recognized what had entered. Silas laid the heartwood on the bench and did not touch it further.

Not yet.

Some things required waiting.

He sat on a stool nearby, elbows on his knees, and studied the grain by lamplight. It twisted and curved in places, refusing symmetry. Fire scars ran through it like darkened veins, impossible to ignore.

He smiled faintly.

Redemption, he knew now, did not erase wounds.

It gave them purpose.

In the days that followed, Silas did not work.

He prayed—not with words, but with patience. He walked. He listened. He allowed grief to settle into gratitude without forcing it to move faster than it could.

His son asked once, "When will you start?"

Silas looked at the wood, then back at the boy.

"When I know what it's meant to become," he said.

The boy thought for a moment. "What if it tells you something you don't want to make?"

Silas smiled sadly. "Then I'll learn obedience again."

One evening, as the valley lay quiet and stars pressed close overhead, Silas felt it.

Not a command.

An invitation.

The shape began to form—not in his hands, but in his heart. Something meant to be held. Passed on. Something that carried story rather than spectacle. Something that could rest in many homes and still speak the same truth.

He placed his hand gently on the heartwood.

"Yes," he whispered.

Outside, the burned forest rested beneath the night sky.

New shoots had already begun to press through ash in places no one expected. Life, it seemed, was never finished—it only waited for the right moment to rise again.

Silas breathed deeply.

The work of redemption had begun.

CHAPTER NINE

THE SHAPING THAT COSTS

Silas learned quickly that choosing the heartwood was the easy part.

Obedience always revealed its true price later—when intention gave way to action, and reverence demanded more than admiration. The wood lay on the bench for days, untouched, as though it were waiting to see whether Silas truly meant what he had promised beneath the fallen tree.

When he finally lifted his tools, his hands trembled—not from doubt of skill, but from the weight of consequence.

This wood would not forgive carelessness.

The first cut was the hardest.

Silas stood for a long time with the plane resting against the grain, eyes tracing the darkened lines where fire had pressed itself into memory. The wood resisted symmetry. It turned unexpectedly, its grain refusing straight answers.

It reminded him uncomfortably of prayer.

He exhaled slowly and followed where the grain led, not where his design preferred. Shavings curled away in thin, fragrant ribbons, falling to the floor like quiet confessions.

Each pass revealed more truth.

Scars widened. Knots emerged. Places Silas might once have hidden now demanded attention. The wood was not interested in appearing whole—it insisted on being honest.

Silas felt something in himself answer that insistence.

Days turned into weeks.

The shaping progressed slowly, interrupted often by long pauses where Silas stepped back, studying the form from every angle. He learned to work only as long as he could remain present. Fatigue bred force. Force bred fracture.

Some evenings, he laid his tools down unfinished, leaving the piece exposed, unresolved. It felt wrong—but necessary.

Redemption, he was learning, could not be rushed.

His son watched closely, sometimes working beside him on smaller projects, sometimes simply sitting quietly near the bench. The boy asked fewer questions now. He had begun to understand that some answers arrived only after waiting had done its work.

One night, after Silas had set his tools aside in visible frustration, the boy spoke softly.

"Does it ever feel like it's shaping you back?"

Silas froze.

He looked at the wood, then at his hands—hands that bore their own scars now, lines etched by years of labor and loss.

"Yes," he said quietly. "That's how you know you're doing it right."

There were moments when Silas doubted himself deeply.

He wondered if he had misunderstood the invitation—if the wood would never become what he sensed it could. There were nights he woke from restless sleep, heart heavy with the fear that he was failing the very legacy he meant to honor.

On those nights, he returned to the workshop alone.

He would run his hand along the grain, feeling the ridges and valleys shaped by fire and storm. He remembered the tree standing tall in wind, absorbing what others could not.

He remembered the warmth still lingering in the trunk after the flames had passed.

And slowly, the doubt loosened.

Not because answers came.

But because faith did.

The piece began to reveal itself.

It was not ornate. It did not demand attention. Its beauty lay in restraint—in the way the form invited touch rather than awe. It fit the hands naturally, as though it had always intended to be held.

Silas smiled when he realized this.

Of course.

Legacy was not something to be displayed.

It was something to be carried.

As the form clarified, the scars found their place.

A long burn mark curved gently along one edge, catching the light just enough to be seen without overwhelming the whole. A knot near the center remained visible, anchoring the piece with quiet authority.

Silas resisted the urge to smooth them away.

He had learned better.

Healing was not the absence of marks.

It was the refusal to let them define the whole.

The work changed Silas.

He found himself slower in speech, more deliberate in judgment. He listened longer. He forgave sooner. The shaping at the bench spilled quietly into the shaping of his heart.

Neighbors noticed.

"You seem lighter," Mara said one afternoon as she stopped by with bread.

Silas considered this. "I think I stopped trying to save what was never meant to stay," he replied.

She nodded, understanding more than he said.

One evening, as the final form neared completion, Silas invited his son to place his hands on the piece.

The boy did so carefully, reverently.

"It feels warm," he said.

Silas smiled. "Some things remember the fire."

The boy looked up. "Will people know what it's made from?"

Silas shook his head. "Not unless they listen closely."

The boy thought for a moment. "Then how will they know it matters?"

Silas placed his hand over his son's shoulder.

"Because it will help them endure," he said. "And that's enough."

The final days of shaping were quiet.

No mistakes. No rushing. Only the steady rhythm of finishing—sanding that softened without erasing, oil that deepened the grain without hiding it.

When Silas finally stepped back, tools laid down for the last time, he felt a mixture of relief and grief.

The work was finished.

And so was a season of becoming.

That night, Silas sat alone in the workshop, the finished piece resting on the bench between light and shadow.

He did not name it.

Some things earned their meaning only when given away.

Outside, the forest stirred gently. New growth pressed upward through ash and soil, slow but determined.

Silas closed his eyes and breathed deeply.

The cost had been real.

But so was the redemption.

CHAPTER TEN

WHAT IS GIVEN AWAY

Silas had always believed that finishing a thing would bring relief.

Instead, when the final coat dried and the piece rested complete upon the bench, he felt a tightening he did not expect—a quiet resistance rising in his chest. The work had shaped him. It had accompanied him through grief and obedience, through nights of doubt and mornings of resolve. Now it asked for the last, most costly act.

"Release".

He understood then why so many things never fulfilled their purpose. Not because they were unfinished—but because they were never given.

The valley gathered without invitation.

Word spread the way it always had—through instinct rather than announcement. People arrived in small numbers at first, then more, standing quietly beneath the open sky where the great tree once stood. Children hushed themselves without being told. Even the wind seemed to move with care.

Silas carried the piece wrapped in cloth, its shape concealed, its weight familiar. His son walked beside him, holding the corner of the fabric as though helping carry something far heavier than wood.

They stopped where the tree's shadow used to fall.

Silas unwrapped the cloth slowly.

The piece did not dazzle. It did not demand admiration. It simply was—honest, warm, marked by scars that had been neither hidden nor exalted. The grain flowed like a map of endured years. Fire's memory lingered, not as damage, but as testimony.

People leaned forward without realizing they had moved.

Silas did not explain.

He had learned that meaning survives best when discovered rather than declared. Instead, he placed the piece into the hands of a child—one whose family had lost everything in the fire, one whose eyes had learned endurance too early.

The child hesitated.

"It's yours," Silas said gently.

The boy looked up. "What is it?"

Silas smiled. "It's what remains."

The child ran his fingers along the grain, tracing the scars with reverent curiosity. Something in his shoulders eased, as though weight had been redistributed without instruction.

A murmur passed through the gathered crowd—not words, but recognition.

In that moment, Silas understood the final shape of faith.

Faith was not just belief held tightly.

It was trust placed carefully.

The tree had given itself to the fire.

The fire had given the heartwood to Silas.

Silas had given the heartwood back to the people.

Nothing had been lost.

It had only changed hands.

Later, as the gathering dispersed and evening settled in, Silas remained behind with his son.

"Does it hurt?" the boy asked quietly.

Silas considered the question honestly.

"Yes," he said. "But not in the way I thought it would."

The boy nodded, accepting this without needing explanation.

They stood together where ash had once smothered the ground. Small green shoots pressed upward now, fragile and determined, claiming space without permission.

"Will you ever make another?" the boy asked.

Silas rested his hand on his son's shoulder. "Maybe. But it won't be the same."

"No," the boy said softly. "Because this one already did what it was meant to do."

Silas smiled.

That night, Silas returned to the workshop alone.

The bench was empty now, bare in a way that felt both unsettling and right. He ran his hand across the surface where the heartwood had rested, half-expecting to feel its warmth linger.

Instead, he felt peace.

He realized then that legacy was never an object.

It was a movement.

Silas slept deeply for the first time in many weeks.

And when he woke, the valley was changed—not restored to what it had been, but alive in a new way. The forest would take years to heal. Some wounds would never close fully.

But the roots were alive.

And what had been given in faith had already begun to bear fruit.

CHAPTER ELEVEN

THE FOREST THAT RISES

Renewal did not arrive with ceremony.

It came the way most true things did—quietly, persistently, without asking permission from what had been lost.

In the weeks after the heartwood was given away, the valley began to change in small, almost unnoticeable ways. Green appeared first in places no one expected. Along the edges of blackened ground, delicate shoots pressed upward, fragile but insistent. Life, it seemed, had been waiting for the right kind of opening.

Silas noticed.

He had learned to.

He walked the valley each morning now, not as a keeper of what once stood, but as a witness to what was becoming. The forest no longer felt empty to him. It felt honest. The scars were visible, yes—but so was the courage of regrowth.

Some people mistook this new beginning for replacement.

Silas knew better.

Nothing was replacing the great tree.

It had simply made room.

Children returned to the clearing where the tree had once stood.

They played differently now—quieter, more intentional, as though they sensed they were standing on something sacred. Silas watched his son kneel beside a patch of new growth, brushing ash away carefully, protecting a cluster of saplings from careless steps.

"What are you doing?" Silas asked.

The boy did not look up. "Helping it to stand."

Silas felt his throat tighten.

The community began to gather again, not beneath branches this time, but around purpose.

People shared tools. They replanted. They rebuilt. Some brought seeds from far places, others used what had survived the fire hidden beneath the soil. No one rushed. They had learned, through loss, that growth hurried rarely endured.

Silas did not lead these efforts.

He stood among them.

Leadership, he had discovered, was not standing in front—it was standing faithfully where work needed doing.

One afternoon, a young man approached Silas hesitantly.

"I remember the tree," he said. "I rested under it once when I had nowhere else to go."

Silas nodded.

"I don't know how to say this," the man continued, voice unsteady. "But that day changed me. I stayed. I endured."

Silas placed a hand on the man's shoulder.

"Then the tree is still standing," he said.

That night, Silas and his son walked the valley together.

Stars pressed close overhead, brighter now without the canopy that once filtered their light. The air smelled of damp soil and promise.

"Do you miss it?" the boy asked.

Silas considered the question carefully.

"Yes," he said. "But I don't feel its absence."

The boy frowned slightly. "How can both be true?"

Silas smiled. "Because what it gave didn't end when it fell."

They stopped near a cluster of saplings growing where the tree's roots had once spread deep and unseen.

Silas knelt and pressed his hand into the soil.

"Everything strong leaves something behind," he said. "Not to replace it—but to continue it."

As seasons passed, Silas aged into a quieter rhythm.

His hands slowed. His workshop filled again—not with urgency, but with invitation. Young ones came to learn. Some stayed. Some moved on, carrying lessons shaped less by instruction and more by example.

Silas taught them how to read grain. How to wait. How to let scars speak.

He never spoke of the fire unless asked.

And even then, he spoke of what followed.

Years later, Silas returned alone to the clearing at dawn.

Saplings now stood taller than he once had when he first knelt beside the wounded tree. Their leaves caught the morning light, trembling slightly in the breeze, learning their own relationship with the wind.

Silas leaned on his staff and smiled.

He did not feel finished.

He felt multiplied.

As the sun rose higher, Silas whispered a prayer without words—a gratitude shaped not by rescue, but by redemption fully received.

He understood now what faith had been teaching him all along:

Nothing given in love is ever truly lost.

It simply changes form—and grows again.

CHAPTER TWELVE

THE GRAIN THAT REMAINS

Silas grew old the way trees do—slowly, almost without notice.

Time did not take him all at once. It thinned his strength before it claimed his days, softened his voice before it quieted his hands. His steps shortened. His breath asked for more pauses. Yet something in him remained deeply rooted, unmoved by the passing years.

He had learned long ago that aging was not a loss of usefulness.

It was a narrowing toward what mattered most.

The workshop grew quieter, though it never emptied.

Silas no longer worked from dawn until dusk. Instead, he chose his hours carefully, giving his strength where it counted. Young hands now filled the space—sons and daughters of the valley, some by blood, many by bond. They came to learn the craft, but stayed for the presence.

Silas taught less with words and more with silence.

He showed them how to wait for the grain to reveal itself. How to set a tool down before impatience could take over. How to tell when a piece of wood had reached its finished truth, even if it did not match the original plan.

"Listen longer than you think you need to," he would say.

"To the wood. To the work. To your own becoming."

His son had grown into a man of steady posture and gentle strength.

Where Silas had once knelt to save a sapling, his son now knelt to guide new growth—teaching children how to plant, how to tend, how to stay. The valley had begun to look to him the way it once had to Silas, not because he asked for it, but because he carried what had been given.

One evening, as the light faded and the forest breathed quietly around them, Silas pressed a familiar object into his son's hands.

The piece made from the heartwood.

Time had deepened its color. Hands had polished it further than oil ever could. Its scars were still visible, still honest, still speaking.

"It's time," Silas said.

His son did not argue.

He understood.

In his final seasons, Silas returned often to the clearing.

The forest there was young now—saplings reaching skyward, roots knitting the soil together again. Birds had returned. Wind moved gently through leaves that had not existed when the fire came.

Silas would sit among them, resting against a trunk not yet wide enough to shelter many, but growing toward that calling all the same.

He placed his hand against the bark and smiled.

Everything he had loved was still here.

On the morning Silas did not rise, the valley felt it.

Not in alarm—but in stillness.

His son found him resting as though he had simply grown tired and stopped walking. There was no struggle written in his face. Only peace, settled deep and sure.

They buried him near the clearing, beneath trees that would one day grow tall enough to carry shadows of their own. No monument was raised. None was needed.

The forest remembered him.

Years later, a child sat beneath a great tree and traced the grain of a wooden object resting in her lap. She did not know Silas's name. She did not know the fire, or the waiting, or the cost of obedience that had shaped what she held.

But she felt something steady there.

Something warm.

Something that helped her endure.

And that was enough.

Because the truth Silas had lived by did not need to be explained to survive:

Strength is formed in hidden places.

Sacrifice is never wasted.

Redemption does not erase the past—it **Redeems** it!

And what is shaped in **Faith**,

What is given in **love**,

What **Endures** the fire and is offered freely—

That grain remains.

EPILOGUE

WHAT THE ROOTS KNOW

Long after Silas was gone, the forest continued its work.

Years softened the scars of fire. Ash became soil. Soil welcomed seed. The land remembered what it had always known—that life does not hurry, and nothing faithful is ever truly erased.

Where the great tree once stood, others now rose. Not one to replace it, but many—each shaped by the same ground, each learning its own conversation with wind and weather. Their roots intertwined beneath the surface, sharing strength in ways unseen by those who passed above them.

If you stood there long enough, you could feel it.

The quiet.

Not emptiness.

Inheritance.

In a home not far from the clearing, a wooden piece rested on a simple table. Time had deepened its color, polished its edges with touch rather than tools. Children traced its grain without knowing why it calmed them. Adults held it during moments when words failed, sensing something steady beneath their uncertainty.

Few knew where it came from.

Fewer still knew what it cost.

But the wood remembered.

Sometimes, on evenings when the valley settled into dusk and the wind moved gently through the trees, someone would pause in the clearing and feel the strange assurance that they were not alone—that something had stood here once, something strong enough to shelter others, something willing to give itself away.

They might not name it as faith.

But they would recognize it.

Because faith, Silas had learned, was never about being spared the fire.

It was about trusting that what passes through the fire can still be made holy.

It was about believing that what is given in love does not disappear—it multiplies. That sacrifice, when received rather than resisted, becomes the seed of renewal. That redemption is not the undoing of pain, but the transformation of it.

And so, the forest grew.

And so, the legacy endured.

Not as a monument carved in stone,

But as strength carried quietly,

As shelter offered without condition,

As roots reaching deeper than memory.

What Silas left behind was never meant to bear his name.

It was meant to bear fruit!

REFLECTION

I did not write this story to explain faith.

I wrote it because faith has spent much of my life explaining me.

There are seasons when belief feels sturdy—like a tree standing tall in good weather. And then there are seasons when fire comes, uninvited and unrelenting, and everything you thought was permanent is tested. What remains after those seasons is never what you expected— but it is often more honest.

Silas was born from that space.

He is not a hero in the way stories often demand. He does not conquer the storm or outrun the fire. He stays. He tends. He waits. He learns that obedience is not always rewarded with preservation, and that love does not guarantee exemption from loss. Yet he also learns something far deeper: that God wastes nothing surrendered in faith.

This story is an allegory, but its truth is practical.

We all tend something.

A calling.

A family.

A marriage.

A craft.

A belief passed down to us by hands now gone.

And at some point, every one of those things will be tested.

The question is not whether the fire will come.

The question is what we believe God can do with what remains.

Scripture tells us that unless a seed falls into the ground and dies, it remains alone. That truth is not poetic—it is costly. Death, in this sense, is rarely sudden. It is often the slow letting go of outcomes we prayed for, the quiet surrender of control, the acceptance that faithfulness does not always look like success.

But it does bear fruit.

Sometimes the fruit is visible: renewal, restoration, new growth rising from ash. Other times it is hidden: strength passed to the next generation, peace that does not depend on circumstances, scars that no longer accuse us of failure but testify to endurance.

Silas learns that redemption does not erase wounds.

It gives them meaning.

If you are reading this while tending something fragile—something bent by storms or marked by fire—I hope this story reminds you that care is never wasted, even when the thing you love does not survive in the form you hoped it would.

What you give in faith does not disappear.

It is carried forward in ways you may never see.

May you have the courage to stay when it would be easier to walk away.

May you learn the patience to follow the grain instead of forcing the cut.

May you trust that what God shapes through endurance is often stronger than what is spared from pain.

And may you believe—especially in the aftermath—that the roots know what the fire cannot destroy.

— Judd R. Johnson

Judd R. Johnson is a craftsman, storyteller, and entrepreneur whose work is rooted in a deep love for woodworking and the quiet beauty of the natural world. Inspired by forests, mountains, and the enduring stories carried within wood and nature, his craft reflects a belief that true meaning is shaped through patience, intention, and respect for the material.

As the founder of TimberTech Heartwood Co., Judd blends traditional craftsmanship with modern storytelling, creating work that honors legacy, resilience, and heartfelt design. Nature remains his greatest teacher, reminding him that growth is not defined by the fire one faces, but by how it forges who we are meant to become.

Through both his writing and his craft, and inspired and encouraged by God and family to record thoughts in its purest form, Judd invites readers to slow down, notice what lasts, and find beauty in what is made by hand, heart and God's creations.